To my boys, Gaang and Sahn

Copyright © 2012 Hyewon Yum
All rights reserved
Color separations by Bright Arts (H.K.) Ltd.
Printed in the United States of America
by Worzalla, Stevens Point, Wisconsin
Designed by Jay Colvin
First edition, 2012
3   5   7   9   10   8   6   4   2

mackids.com

Library of Congress Cataloging-in-Publication Data
Yum, Hyewon.
     Mom, it's my first day of kindergarten! / Hyewon Yum. — 1st ed.
          p.   cm.
     Summary: A five-year-old boy, ready and eager on his first day at "the big
kids' school," must calm his very worried mother.
     ISBN 978-0-374-35004-8
     [1. First day of school—Fiction.   2. Kindergarten—Fiction.
3. Schools—Fiction.   4. Worry—Fiction.   5. Mothers and sons—Fiction.]
I. Title.   II. Title: Mom, it is my first day of kindergarten!

PZ7.Y89656Mom 2012
[E]—dc23
                                                                    2011018294

MOM, IT'S MY FIRST DAY OF KINDERGARTEN!

HYEWON YUM

FRANCES FOSTER BOOKS

FARRAR STRAUS GIROUX

NEW YORK

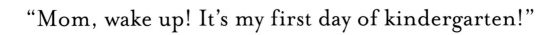

"Mom, wake up! It's my first day of kindergarten!"

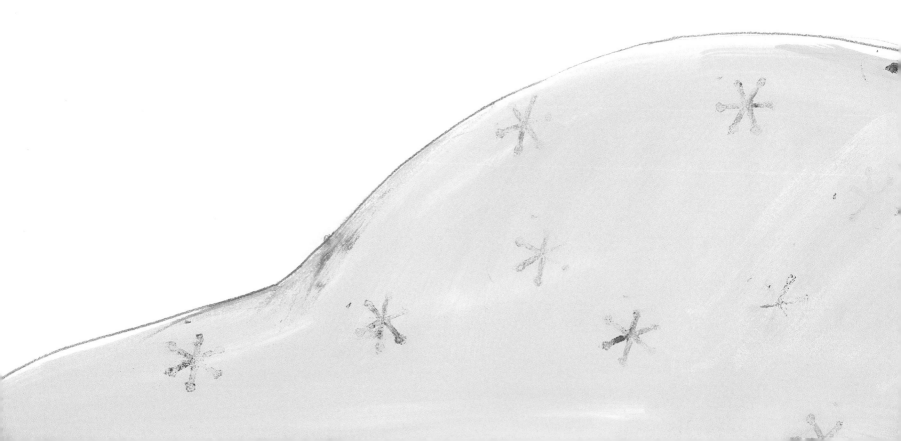

Mom makes my lunch and she starts to worry. "Do they have snacks in kindergarten? What if you don't have time to finish your sandwich at lunch? You'll be so hungry."

"I can eat fast, Mom."

"Did I pack all your school supplies? What if I forgot something?"
She worries and worries.

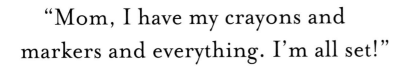

"Mom, I have my crayons and markers and everything. I'm all set!"

"Oh dear! Look at the time, you'll be late for school."

"Don't worry, Mom. We can run!"

"Will you be okay in the big kids' school?
You're still so little."

"Mom, don't worry. I'll be fine, I am already five!"

"Oh, it's such a big school. You could get lost here."

"Mom, it's not that big. I think it's just right for a big boy like me."

Mom doesn't look happy.
"We don't know anyone here. I miss your old teachers and your friends."

"I like to make new friends, Mom, and you'll make new friends, too, in no time."

I say hi to the girl with a pink ribbon.
She says hi.

And her mom says hi to my mom.
My mom smiles back.

We find my classroom.
The door is open.
"Uh-oh, Mom, maybe I'm not
ready for this."

Mom sighs. "I'm sure you'll be fine in kindergarten," she says.

Then my teacher comes out to greet us. She smiles and says,
"Hello, are you ready for kindergarten?"
And then, I know . . .

"Oh, yes, I am ready for kindergarten! I've been waiting for this all summer. I'm five. It's time for me to go to the big kids' school."

And I walk right into the classroom.

When my teacher says parents should leave, Mom hugs me, and kisses me, and hugs me, and kisses me.

I say, "Bye."

Then we get to work.
Kindergarten is awesome.

I spend all day with my new friends. Before I know it, it's time to go home.

When we line up, I feel so much bigger.

We follow our teacher out to the school yard.
And there's Mom, waiting for me.

I hug her, and she hugs me.

"How was school?" she asks.

"It's awesome," I say.

"You're right, you're just the right size for the big kids' school. I'm so proud of you!" Mom says.
And I tell her all about my first day of kindergarten.

"Mom, can I take the school bus tomorrow, please?"
"Oh dear."

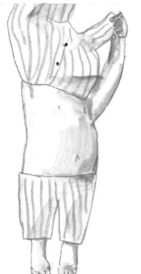